Table of Contents

Rourke Educational Media
A Division of Carson Dellosa Education
rourkeeducationalmedia.com

Can you find these words?

owner

paws

puppies

wolves

German Shepherd Puppies

These are German Shepherd **puppies!**

What do German Shepherd puppies look like?

They look like **wolves**.

They have large **paws.**

paws

They get big. They grow to 24 inches (61 centimeters) tall.

What do German Shepherd puppies act like? They are smart.

They can learn to be police dogs.

They make good friends.

They stay close to their **owner**.

Did you find these words?

They stay close to their **owner**.

They have large **paws**.

These are German Shepherd **puppies**!

They look like **wolves**.

Photo Glossary

owner (OHN-ur): Someone who possesses or has something.

paws (pawz): The feet of animals that have four legs and claws.

puppies (PUHP-eez): Dogs that are young and not fully grown.

wolves (wulvz): Wild animals related to dogs.

Index

About the Author

Hailey Scragg is a writer from Ohio. She loves all puppies, especially her puppy, Abe! She likes taking him on long walks in the park.

www.rourkeeducationalmedia.com

PHOTO CREDITS: cover: ©Nine_Tomorrows, ©manley099 (bone); back cover: ©YSimoneau (inset), ©Naddiya (pattern); pages 2, 3, 14, 15: ©Bigandt_Photography; pages 4-5: ©Vera Zinkova; pages 2, 5, 14, 15: ©Karel Bartik; pages 2, 6-7, 14, 15: ©Grigorita Ko; pages 8-9: ©Julia Shepeleva; page 10: ©BiancaGrueneberg; page 11: ©NSC Photography; pages 2, 12-13, 14, 15: ©Dariia Pavlova

Edited by: Kim Thompson
Cover and interior design by: Janine Fisher

Library of Congress PCN Data
German Shepherd Puppies / Hailey Scragg
(Top Puppies)
ISBN 978-1-73162-870-1 (hard cover)(alk. paper)
ISBN 978-1-73162-869-5 (soft cover)
ISBN 978-1-73162-871-8 (e-Book)
ISBN 978-1-73163-344-6 (ePub)
Library of Congress Control Number: 2019945031

Printed in the United States of America,
North Mankato, Minnesota